Dedicated to all artists—past, present, and future—
who bring the characters and love of *Sesame Street* to vibrant life

SUNNY DAY

A Celebration of SESAME STREET

music by
JOE RAPOSO

words by

BRUCE HART,
JON R. STONE
& JOE RAPOSO

Random House New York

Sunny day,

Sweepin' the clouds away.

On my way

To where the air

is sweet.

Can you tell me how to get,

how to get to Sesame Street?

Come and play!

Everything's A-OK.

Friendly neighbors there,

that's where we meet.

Can you tell me how to get,

how to get to Sesame Street?

It's a magic carpet ride.
Every door will open wide

To happy people like you,

happy people like you.

What a beautiful

sunny day,

sweepin' the clouds away.

On my way to where

the air is sweet.

Can you tell me how to get,

how to get to Sesame Street?

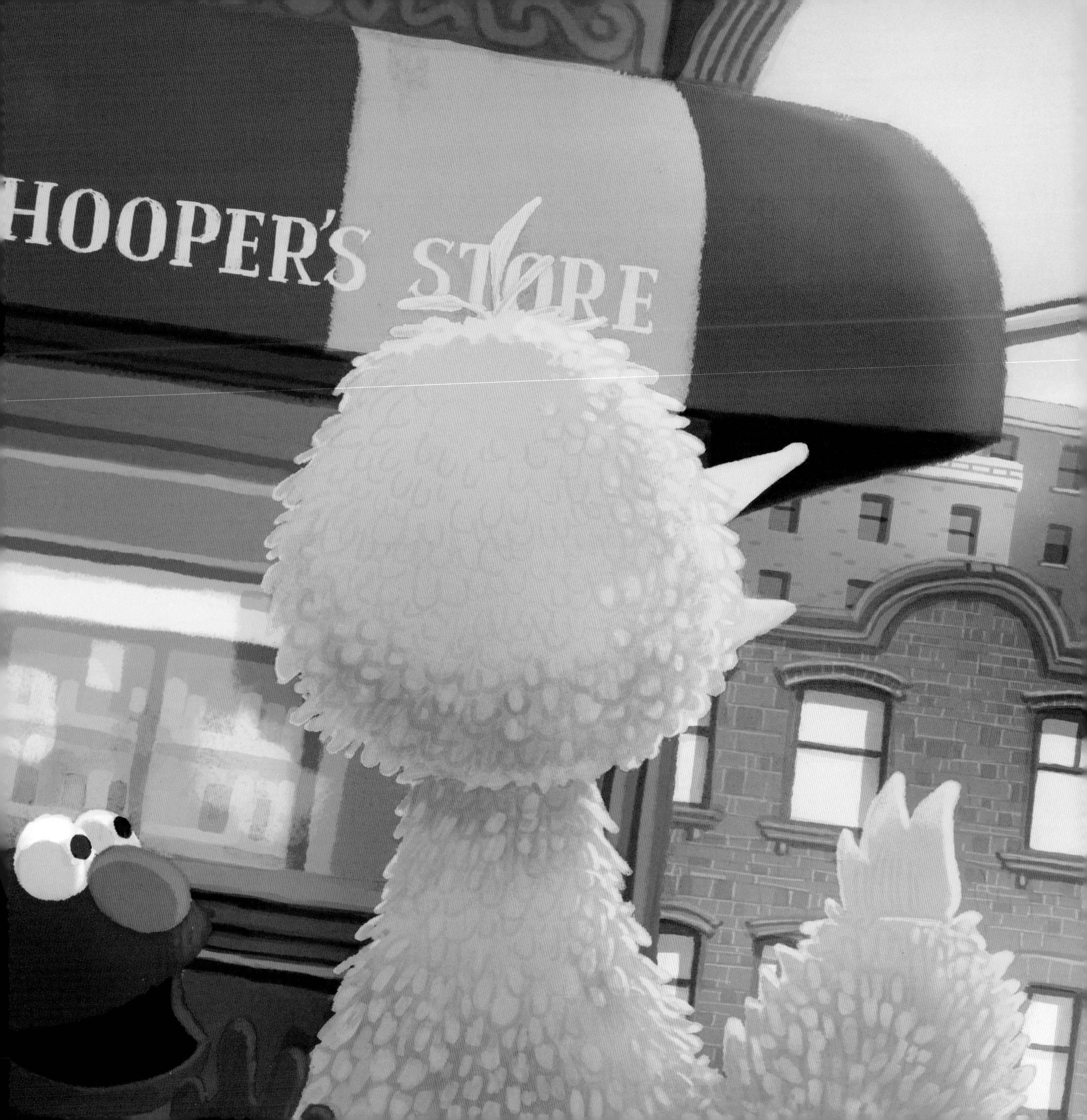
HOOPER'S STORE

How to get to

Sesame Street?

CONTRIBUTORS (in order of appearance)

CHRISTIAN ROBINSON (jacket) is an author and illustrator of books for children. He illustrated the *New York Times* bestseller *Last Stop on Market Street* by Matt de la Peña, which was awarded a Caldecott Honor and the Newbery Medal. A graduate of the California Institute of the Arts, he is a former animator who has worked with Sesame Workshop and Pixar Animation Studios. Christian is based in Sacramento, California. Follow @TheArtofFunNews on Twitter and Instagram.

Photo credit: Anastasiia Sapon

ROGER BRADFIELD (case cover) is an illustrator, comic-strip creator, and commercial artist who illustrated some of the earliest *Sesame Street* books in the 1970s. At the time, *Sesame Street* artists were free to create their own style, and Bradfield's is distinctive and memorable. He retired in 1988 and lives in California with his family. Visit rogerbradfield.com.

ZIYUE CHEN (endpapers) is a Singapore-based illustrator and a graduate of the Ringling College of Art and Design. Through her illustrations, she seeks to establish an emotional connection with those who view her work. She recalls, "*Sesame Street* gave me fond memories of my fascination with colorful animated numbers and letters during my childhood." Visit ziyuechen.com.

JOE MATHIEU (title page) drew his first caricature at age eleven and went on to become an artist and professional illustrator. In a prolific career, he has created art for hundreds of children's books—among them Dr. Seuss titles— as well as album covers (he favors jazz). Joe began illustrating *Sesame Street* books the year they first appeared, in 1971, and is still at it. Visit joemathieu.com.

Photo credit: Marc Andrews Stephens

TOM LICHTENHELD creates books for children and for people who used to be children. The *New York Times* bestselling picture books *Goodnight, Goodnight, Construction Site* by Sherri Duskey Rinker and *I Wish You More* by Amy Krouse Rosenthal are just two of the many books featuring his trademark humor and warmth. Tom resides near Chicago. Visit tomlichtenheld.com, and follow @tlichtenheld on Twitter.

SEAN QUALLS finds inspiration all around. He's a self-taught artist and illustrator, and his books and illustrations often explore history and nonfiction subjects. His fine art focuses on race and identity and the intersection of history and mythology. Together his paintings and illustrations reveal simultaneously unique and universal moments that portray the human spirit. His recent books include *Why Am I Me?* by Paige Britt, *The Case for Loving* by Selina Alko, and *Two Friends* by Dean Robbins, all of which he illustrated with Selina Alko, his wife. His awards and honors include the Schneider Family Book Award and a Coretta Scott King Honor Award. He lives with his family in Brooklyn, New York. Visit seanqualls.com.

Photo credit: Ted Lewis

Photo credit: Goodjob.com

SELINA ALKO grew up in a house filled with books and paintings. She remembers watching *Sesame Street* as a child and admiring the way the diverse characters in the neighborhood coexisted. Now the award-winning author-illustrator spends her days blending words and mixed-media art to convey stories of hope and inspiration—as well as an alternative viewpoint. She lives in neighborly Brooklyn, New York, with her artist husband, Sean Qualls. Visit selinaalko.com, and follow @SelinaAlko on Twitter and Instagram.

EMILY WINFIELD MARTIN is a fine artist and author-illustrator of children's books, including the *New York Times* bestselling *The Wonderful Things You Will Be.* Her work is inspired by fairy tales, music, myths, classic illustrations, her favorite films, and the natural world. She lives in Portland, Oregon. Follow @MsEmilyApple on Twitter and @emilyblackapple on Instagram.

Photo credit: Josiah Shoup

Photo credit: Yuchung Chao

JOEY CHOU was born in Taiwan and moved to sunny California in his early teens. There he received his BFA from ArtCenter College of Design. After moving to the United States, Joey watched a lot of *Sesame Street* to help him learn English. His favorite characters are Big Bird and Cookie Monster. Joey works as a visual development artist on animated feature films, including *Hotel Transylvania* and *Cloudy with a Chance of Meatballs.* He has illustrated numerous picture books in his distinctive graphic style, which is influenced by many great illustrators who were working in the 1960s, such as Mary Blair, Alice and Martin Provensen, and Ezra Jack Keats. Visit joeyart.com, and follow @choochoojoey on Instagram.

KENARD PAK lives in the hills of San Francisco with his wife and cats. A graduate of Syracuse University and a former animator, Ken likes to think about hills, clouds, rain, and animals when he draws and writes. His awards and other honors include the Golden Kite Award for Picture Book Illustration for *Goodbye Autumn, Hello Winter.* In his free time, he watches baseball and bikes to the park. Follow @Kenardpak on Instagram and Twitter.

RAFAEL LÓPEZ uses his hands and imagination to create award-winning children's books and murals around the world. *The Day You Begin* by Jacqueline Woodson debuted at number one on the *New York Times* bestseller list, and *Maybe Something Beautiful* by F. Isabel Campoy and Theresa Howell was chosen as a Read for the Record Book. Rafael has won numerous awards for his illustrations, including two Pura Belpré Awards, two Américas Awards, the Society of Illustrators Original Art Silver Medal, and the Tomás Rivera Mexican American Book Award. He lives in San Diego and in San Miguel de Allende, Mexico. Visit rafaellopez-books.com, and follow @Rafael_161 on Instagram and @rafaellopezart on Twitter.

PAT CUMMINGS is the author and/or illustrator of more than thirty-five books for young readers. She also edited the award-winning series Talking with Artists, which profiles prominent children's book illustrators. Her classes at Parsons School of Design and Pratt Institute have a growing number of notable author-illustrators among their graduates. Pat serves on the boards of the Authors Guild, the Authors League Fund, and the Society of Children's Book Writers and Illustrators, and she chairs the Society of Illustrators' Original Art Founder's Award. She lives in Brooklyn, New York, with her husband, H. Chuku Lee, who wrote the text for her recent picture book *Beauty and the Beast*. Pat credits *Sesame Street* for providing a profound life lesson about making choices via Ernie's moving rendition of "Put Down the Duckie," although she does *not* play the saxophone. Visit patcummings.com.

BRIGETTE BARRAGER is an artist, character designer, illustrator, and author. She is best known for illustrating the *New York Times* bestselling picture books *Uni the Unicorn* and *Uni the Unicorn and the Dream Come True* by Amy Krouse Rosenthal. Brigette works in Los Angeles, where she lives with her handsome husband, who can sometimes be found among the characters in her books. Follow @missbrigette on Instagram.

VANESSA BRANTLEY-NEWTON is an illustrator, doll maker, and crafter who studied fashion illustration at the Fashion Institute of Technology and children's book illustration at the School of Visual Arts. She makes her nest in Charlotte, North Carolina, with her husband, their daughter, and a very rambunctious cat named Stripes. Visit vanessabrantleynewton.com, and follow @vanessabrantleynewton on Instagram.

MIKE CURATO is the creator of everyone's favorite polka-dotted elephant, Little Elliot, who garnered him a Flying Start designation from *Publishers Weekly* and a Society of Illustrators Original Art Founder's Award. In addition to the five books about this cupcake-loving elephant, Mike has illustrated several other books, including *Worm Loves Worm* by J. J. Austrian. As a kid, Mike loved the *Sesame Street* segment about how crayons are made. As an adult, he still knows all the words to Oscar the Grouch's song "I Love Trash," and he enjoyed using materials that some people might consider trash to create his illustration for this book! Mike lives in Northampton, Massachusetts, and shares Little Elliot's passion for cupcakes. Visit mikecurato.com, and follow @mikecurato on Twitter and @mike_curato on Instagram.

Photo credit: Dylan Osborne

LEO ESPINOSA is an award-winning illustrator and designer from Bogotá, Colombia. His work has been featured in a variety of publications, products, animated series, and gallery shows worldwide. A short list includes the *New Yorker, Wired, Esquire,* the *New York Times,* the *Atlantic,* Nickelodeon, Hasbro, American Greetings, Coca-Cola, and Facebook. Leo's illustrations have been recognized by *American Illustration, Communication Arts, 3x3,* Pictoplasma, and the Society of Illustrators. In addition, he has given many lectures and workshops at schools and institutions—such as Parsons School of Design, Pratt Institute, and the Rhode Island School of Design. Leo lives with his family in Salt Lake City. Visit studioespinosa.com.

Photo credit: Josh Blumental

GREG PIZZOLI is the author and/or illustrator of a number of picture books. He wrote and illustrated *Tricky Vic: The Impossibly True Story of the Man Who Sold the Eiffel Tower,* a *New York Times* Best Illustrated Book of the Year, and illustrated *Crunch, the Shy Dinosaur* by Cirocco Dunlap. Greg lives on a very friendly street in Philadelphia. Visit gregpizzoli.com.

DAN SANTAT, author–illustrator of numerous award-winning picture books, may be best known for *The Adventures of Beekle: The Unimaginary Friend,* which won the Caldecott Medal. He has illustrated over eighty-five other books for children, some of which he also wrote, such as *Are We There Yet?* and *After the Fall.* Dan lives in Southern California with his wife, their two kids, and an assortment of pets. Visit dantat.com, and follow @dsantat on Twitter.